T0143003

UNCLE JERRY -
Pedophiles invited in your House

UNCLE JERRY -
Pedophiles invited in your House

The Advocate

iUniverse

UNCLE JERRY - PEDOPHILES INVITED IN YOUR HOUSE

iUniverse books may be ordered through booksellers or by contacting:

iUniverse
1663 Liberty Drive
Bloomington, IN 47403
www.iuniverse.com
844-349-9409

Because of the dynamic nature of the Internet, any web addresses or links contained in this book may have changed since publication and may no longer be valid. The views expressed in this work are solely those of the author and do not necessarily reflect the views of the publisher, and the publisher hereby disclaims any responsibility for them.

Any people depicted in stock imagery provided by Getty Images are models, and such images are being used for illustrative purposes only. Certain stock imagery © Getty Images.

ISBN: 978-1-6632-1566-6 (sc)
ISBN: 978-1-6632-1567-3 (e)

Library of Congress Control Number: 2021901900

Print information available on the last page.

iUniverse rev. date: 01/29/2021

DEDICATION

This book is to Thank my mother (Mattie Bea) and father (Adolph Eady Sr.) for coming together to create LinNette Eady and Adolph Eady Jr. LinNette Eady created Regina Renee' Eady (only Child) she created Jamica Joy Eady, William Eady (Poo) and Bethany Curtis. Adolph Eady Jr. created Shawn Meadows and Andrei Meadows. And the list goes on and on. I am a great-grand mother of 8 and one on the way.

There are not many of us - but the name and blood of the Eady clan is more powerful than tribes of others. Would not trade my name "Eady" ever.

The Advocate

After writing "Portrait of a Rape" I have talked to several women that told me that the beginning of their sexual trauma began as a child. I remembered Uncle Jerry fondling me at the young age of 4. I would play with Uncle Jerry for hours. He would tickle me and I would laugh. He would bounce me on his knee. He would say "ride em pony". I remember him touching me all the time. This book is written about pedophiles in your house and around your children. Although its' content is mostly directed for women, however, there more and more men raising their children alone.

I had to do extensive research on the subject about pedophiles and their behavior. It is vast information on the internet, so you can do your own research. Hopefully, this book will encourage you to be aware of who is around your children. Not only your girls but little boys can become a victim of Uncle Jerry.

UNCLE JERRY – PEDOPHILES AROUND YOUR CHILDREN

The reason this book is important.

So many women lone for the touch of a man. We are brought up in families that don't know how to love or express love. We are brought up in families without a male figure to show us how love looks. We see mothers being mistreated verbally or physically. We are being beat by our parents and never hugged or told we are loved. As human being we need to be touched and held and cuddled to feel secure. We need to hear; "I love you" from our parents. But we see our single mothers searching for love by several different men. Searching disparately for security. Needing

a tender touch hoping the whispers of lies are true. "I love you"; "You are the only one for me"; "You feel so good to me"; "I missed you so much"; "I love the way you make me feel"; "I'm gonna make you mine"; "We will get married soon" and many other lies. Those with No or Low self-esteem fall as easy prey to the deceitful technics practiced by these predators for centuries. The same old game with different victims one after another. Don't feel bad if you were a victim of this hurtful game.

Men that have not been shown love growing up, don't know how to show love. Some men show love by beating women. Some men show love by verbal or physical abuse. Don't be fooled, verbal abuse is just as harmful, if not worse than physical abuse; a broken arm may heal but harmful words last forever and kills self-esteem. Other men keep searching for love with several women; not finding love at all but creating babies without a

father figure. They imitate love by saying the right things that women want to hear. Always look at their action and the way you feel after they leave your presence. If you feel sad, worthless, lonely, tired, drained after he leaves, he is probably going to his next victim, run. The signs are usually clear but the need to be love overwhelms your senses and you began to swirl in a trance and expose your family to a pedophile's playground. Protect your babies.

The numbers change every year on the number of victims of pedophiles. This book is a guideline for women but men can find it helpful. Single women with the complicated task of raising children by themselves can use this information as a guideline to protest their children in this complicated society in the midst of various types of mental illness. Beware of the friendly faces around your precious and innocent children.

If drugs and/or alcohol is involved the level of exposure increases ten-fold.

There is usually a stranger in our home around our children and you let them sit in Uncle Jerry's lap. He watches your children while you go to work or let them go to the store with them. Freedom to pick and choose the next victim of their untamed lust. There is a pedophile among us. They come friendly and baring gifts. Some don't have money but swept the lady of the house off her feet with fantastic sexual acts, leaving her children available for the unsatisfied lust that consume him or her. Beware before inviting monsters into your life, they don't want you; they want your little girls or little boys.

My daughter lived behind an alley. On the way to the store, her boyfriend noticed there was a car rocking in the alley. Upon looking into

the car there was a man having sex with a child. Pound on a child and destroy her soul. When asked what he was doing his reply was; "Just taking care of my business" "Mine your business". When the police arrived, he was gone and car was reported stolen. Watch your children even though you may be sexually active and have desires try to keep your sexual life separate. Sometimes the predator might be the natural father. Drugs and alcohol can cause sexual assault because the mind is distorted and actions are performed in a blackout state.

It is not a good idea to bring people that do drugs and drink excessively around your children. Do a background check before you get involved. The altered state of mind of predators causes misjudgment and bad decisions; like molesting your children. These predators hunt to devour families. If they molest your child, they may

have sex with the whole family leaving the family ties destroyed. Having sex with you, your sister, mother and aunts. If he is a real pervert he may have down-low sex with your brother and uncles. Beware of the predator sign. Showing too much interest in your children or their age. Taking them to the store alone, being gone too long. Volunteering to babysit is another sign of sexual lust. Roaming around the house at night, being gone too long may be an hour of terror for your child. Strange behavior from your children and been scare to be alone with him is a tell-tale sign that something is wrong. Crawling up in his lap right in front of you should not be allowed. All these acts are magnified with drugs and alcohol. Protect your children and protect your family from outside or inside predators.

The Uncle Jerrys of our society may wear a disguise of being a coach, teacher, preacher,

minister, deacons, members of choir, members of church that shout the loudest, priest, good neighbor, boy scout/girl scout leader, camp leader, military personnel, trusted friend, lover, long-time friend of family, drunks, dope addicts, someone is always around. You should put up hidden camera to see what's going on in your house. Screen your child's friends and be careful about overnight stays. Know who is in that house. The brother or his friend could be a young predator in the making. It may sound like being paranoid, but be aware. This world now is a dangerous place. There is a large percentage of women that have been sexually assaulted in childhood or as adults that never told their story nor received treatment. It is expected of them to be quite and hold all that pain and sorrow so they will not mess up the predator's life, yet the woman goes to their grave with the tremendous burden of horror, terror and

pain. It is expected in this society somehow it is her fault. It is expected that she is strong while she holds back the tears on a daily basis. She recalls the day her mother makes her call a stranger daddy as he molests her weekly. She recalls the threats whispered in her ear about killing her family as this man finds pleasure in this innocent virgin child. Abnormal behavior is a result of childhood trauma. Some of these innocent little girls hate men so much they resort to homosexually. The predators are always around teaching your child about sex while they are way too young.

It was always thought this can only happen to little girls. The little boys are victims too. Evil does not discriminate between male and female. A drunken pervert will have sex with a little boy as quick as a little girl. Sometime they are not drunk just have a sickness and lust that is uncontrollable. They break the spirit of the little boy and the child

becomes submissive to this terrible act. Because society endorses man and woman and not man with man or woman with woman the male child that has been messed with finds it hard to be accepted in society, however things are changing. When a man is raped, the psychological effects are extremely devasting. The genre change can have a life-long affect. Confusion about their role and purpose in life can prevent them from having a full whole life. Trauma last forever. The way it is processed can help one make it through.

Uncle Jerry is having fun messing up children's life for his pleasure. The sickness of it all. The excuse it was done to him is no excuse. Unfortunately, there is no class on what is right and what is wrong in love making, there is no class on how to love, thus divorce is very high because we are not taught how to love and show it properly. Most households lost the value of

eating together to discuss basic manners and how to be kind to one another. No instructions on how to resolve problems. No sexual classes within the home. We spoil our children by giving them whatever they want without making them earn it. We want our children to have more than we had, thus creating a monster. Now, when they can't have what they want, they throw a temper tantrum and take it. This behavior can crossover into taking sex creating a rapist. She said no, I will take it anyway. Being imprinted with the behavior created by parents to give your child anything he/she asked for and the pattern continues into adulthood. Or, the child that didn't have anything and shown no affection, starving for attention demands attention from an unwilling source. Forcing an unwilling victim into unwilling sex, is still a rapist. Uncle Jerrys are created in so many ways; yet they bring great

harm to their victims even though they may be victims themselves. We have a duty to talk to our children about sex and love. Sex is not voodoo or a bad thing, it is when it is not consensual, both parties agree to participate in a sexual activity. Teach them about love and how to Love. When a child grows up in a household where they can't see love and feel love their feeling are more based on lust than feelings. Love is more of an intense feeling of deep affection which include physical and emotional attachment' Love is something more than a lust in the loin (sexual organs – source of erotic or procreative power).

MANNERS ARE IMPORTANT BUT ACTIONS CAN DESTROY

If we are taught manners as a child we might understand and respect No means NO and respect that as No Sex. There are women out there that tease men and end up being rape. This is not fair for the innocent woman that fall victims of a horrible crime. A man can become so enraged that the act takes on more violence. If he is brought up in a violent household hitting and beating can go along with the rape. Most of the family friends will use threats to intimidate a child. Threats to get their younger sister, threats to kill a family member or other types on intimidations. Children are very vulnerable; their innocence can be used

to multiplate them. When the assault comes from a close family member or sibling all trust is destroyed. Ensure your child that they can tell you anything and they don't have to keep anything from you. Keep an open communication so your child can tell you if Uncle Jerry is touching them inappropriately. Don't try to scare them into telling you, talk gently and kind, they are already scared Uncle Jerry might kill you. Such a heavy burden for a young child to carry. Set aside some me and you time for your child to enjoy their childhood, they grow up fast. Teach them by showing respect for others. Your actions are what they follow. If they see you smoking, they probably will, too. If they hear you cussing all the time, they probably will, too. If they see the father beating the mother, they probably will beat their mate, too. If they see the mother with many men, they probably will do the same, the pattern go from generation to generation.

They see their mother struggling on food stamps and several baby daddies, they might follow in her footstep because they don't know any better and did not see better. Know your responsibility as a parent is to be a parent NOT A FRIEND. If you become friends after being a parent that is excellent and a plus.

ACTUAL EVENTS

I read a story about an Uncle Jerry coming to visit this family and everyday he would put his finger in this three-year-old child. After a while he would put two fingers in her to ready her for his entry. By the time he could put three fingers in her she was ready for his penis. He got too relaxed and was caught by the mother. He was the grandfather. Uncle Jerry was in the family, be careful.

I read another case where the brother continued having sex with is baby sister for years and finally, she got pregnant and the DNA discovered he was the father. The parents let them sleep together because they could not afford a bigger apartment so they could have separate bedrooms. The parent

UNCLE JERRY - Pedophiles invited in your House

became suspicious when they noticed they was sleeping late and going to bed early, with the door shut. Children should not have their door shut while staying in your house.

9

TEACH YOUR CHILD SKILLS TO PROTECT THEMSELF

I wish there was a book on how to be a parent, but it is not. There are some precautions to outline on things to teach your child. Manners are big, being polite, holding door for elders, no cussing around elders, sharpen communication skills with listening being the key factor, and learning to earn your allowance instead of always giving them money without earning it. You can meet someone and tell if they had a decent bring up. Manners are still cute. Being polite is not old fashion. Going to school or reading a book is not out of style. Knowledge is King but Wisdom is the highest form of being a human being. Teach your child how to mediate. Teach your child that it is

ok to exercise; don't let them spend hours looking at on-line show to babysit your child. Some of those shows are teaching some bad habits. Uncle Jerry is looking at them too. They can entice your child and will start up conservation with these innocent children for their sexual pleasure. There are so many Uncle Jerrys online nowadays lurking to find that lonely child and bounce on them like a lion in heat. With the abundance of online traps for the children and the defiance of our teenagers, parents need to establish some guideline and pray. They can become victims and start on a road to becoming an Uncle Jerry or Aunt Jane.

AUNT JANES

Don't think it is only Uncle Jerrys that infuriate families, Aunt Janes have found pleasure in families that introduce sex to young boys, too. Some thinks it's cute for a young 10 years old to have sex early. The act and smells for a very young boy can have a life-long trauma on his mental state of mind. He may not understand some girls may not want to experiment with him. The feeling of sex may be so strong that an Uncle Jerry has been created too young to understand "NO". The predator was created before he could understand love and affection, just pure pleasure. I've asked men about their first encounter and some told me that Aunt Jane opened up her legs and told me to lick it. After several times licking it and getting used to the smell she told me to

stick my penis in her and when I tried to pull away, she forced me to keep it in her until she got really wet. They were traumized when they had an organism, not knowing what was happening to them, but learned to love it, with or without consent. So little boys can get raped without knowing what is going on. Don't sleep on Aunt Jean, she is a sexual predator, too.

NO more HUSH-HUSH about family secrets

The realization that sexual predators are among us must be confronted head on. We can no longer turn a blind eye to this threat. The internet makes it so easy for their conquest. Pretending to be a child of the same age they gain their confidence with your child. They find out secrets from your child and the rest in history.

Check to see what sites your child visited and what screen names were used. There have been many cases of children meeting their new friend only to find their new friend is over 18 and much older. Many children end up kidnaped and part of an international sex ring. Their poor bodies used for the pleasure of several Uncle Jerrys all across the world. Several are given drugs to make them numb to the sexual assault. Their DNA changes to make them into someone you will never recognize. What would make this world so cruel? We must protect our children. Drugs can be a big factor in the selling of children. There have been many cases of selling children for just a few dollars. It is a big responsibility to raise a child in such a difficult world. There are actually some children that are molested by their biological parents and the risk becomes great with a step-child. The conscientious of some

men are void when it comes to sex. The urge to have that two-minute feeling of ejaculation into a virgin is sickening. I can't imagine hours of pounding on a baby and them finding pleasure. Even more sickening is the thought of baby boys going through the same thing. In actuality, sex is designed for procreation only. Somewhere along the line men, have made the act of creating life to pure pleasure. Most species have sex to procreate not for pleasure.

TYPES OF SEXUAL PREDATORS

The term *Post Coital Dysphoria* is to explain the emotional issue after sex for someone where there is no real feelings of pleasure. After sex there is an empty void feeling. Sex without intimacy. There can be a connection after been molested as a child because there is no mature connection with the sex partner. Religious believes make one think that sex is bad. A childhood rape interferes with a long-term relationship as an adult. Men can feel guilty about their sexual misconduct and use the body image as a wedge between partners. If your sexual partner is not a gentle lover or not attentive to your needs post coital dysphoria may occur and leave you sexually frustrated. Communication may be the first step in improving your sexual

encounters with your partner. If early sexual encounters were exploiting a child the problem is deep rooted and therapy may be necessary. Sometimes depression and anxiety can interfere with one's sex life. The anxiety and depression can be brought on by guilty feelings from past behaviors.

Compulsive Sexual behavior is a condition that keep sexual thoughts about sex that interfere with ability to maintain relationships, daily routines, and cannot manage their sexual behavior. This behavior is also been called sexual addiction. This is a mental health issue. This behavior can develop into sexual impulses so strong that the acts of sex is done over and over. This Uncle is sick and no child or adult female is safe around him, he can't hear "NO", this condition causes changes in the pre-frontal cortex that controls judgement, learning, decision making and behavior control.

The urges in this area of the brain causing the repetitive sexual behavior. This statement is no excuse for bad behavior.

Uncle Jerry is somewhat of a sociopath, only thinking of his pleasure without feeling the pain and destruction of a family or life of the child he has destroyed. Self-centered and void of feeling, what a dangerous combination. He may be having some remorse and a guilty feeling with a weak conscience. Sociopaths have excuse for their behavior and always blame someone else for their bad behavior. They act without thinking. Most have a Narcissistic personality disorder which have an excessive need for attention and admiration to feed their ego. They also have a grandiose sense of self-importance. Their sense of entitlement makes them think they have the right to have sex with whomever they want and children is no exception. A psychopathic narcissist

may become extremely violet and can become a serial killer because they can't get their way. And you invite this kind of person in your house and around your family. Your children are the most valuable object of his blizzard delusion. Again, protect your children from this predator.

A pedophile is a person that is attracted to children. This is a psychiatric disorder where adult or older adolescent of the age of 16 are attract to children. This too is a mental disorder. *Ephebophilia* are interested in children 15 to 19. *Paraphilia* tends to want extreme sex with dangerous acts. *Voyeurism* likes to watch naked people to get sexual pleasure. *Masochism* likes to insert pain or humiliation to find sexual pleasure. *Sadism* love to belittle victim by using pain, very similar to them masochist.

The point here is there are several sexual disorders that hide in people. Be careful who you

let into your house and around your children. Don't bring an Uncle Jerry into your house and let your children run around the house with no clothes on. This can get him aroused. I know you may have sexual needs but don't let him blow your mind with good sex while his mind is on your child down the hall. Nowadays you may have to worry about the boys, too.

UNCLE JERRY WOULDN'T HURT A FLY

Uncle Jerry presents themselves has funny, helpful, thoughtful, kind, sweet and "could hurt a fly" type guy. They come to devour your whole family. They are always around. Don't let your children be alone with him. Do not let your children sit in his lap. Keep him out your house. Protect your family from these predators. It's time to build stronger family ties. Let's start reading together again and have a topic to share around the dinner table. Teach each of your children how to identify unwanted touching. Tell you children Uncle Jerry is not going to kill your family. Uncle Jerry tell your children he is going to kill their mother, father, sister or brother if they tell what

they are doing to them. So, the child suffers in silence. A huge burden for such a little soul. They act out because they cannot tell anyone. Their growth is stunt at such a young age. How do you think they feel, seeing their family members laughing and talking to Uncle Jerry that have dark secrets and not sharing secret thing of a sexual nature? Uncle Jerry stole his/her childhood and made that child desire a feeling for him that is unnatural. The brain does not fully develop until around 25 years old, so decisions made before then are immature. This is a sick situation. Your poor child; ask questions and try to keep the child from being afraid to talk to you. Create a safe zone, a time to let your child share secrets, desires and expressions. If your child is scare of you and scare of Uncle Jerry they may turn to drugs, the pimping Uncle Jerry, alcohol or worst. Look for

signs, acting out, sleeping a lot, scares from sucky marks. Check your child's complete body.

Now, let's talk about Self-esteem. The meaning of self-esteem is confidence in one's own worth or abilities; and self-respect. The reason this chapter is so important is Uncle Jerry seeks out women with low self-esteem. The first love is to love yourself. If you love yourself you will not allow anyone to disrespect you.

Self-respect is essential in decision making. If you don't respect yourself; no one else will. Access the situation before you make a decision in your life that will have a lasting effect on your life.

Men seek women with low self-esteem to feed their deflated ego. I know women let men into their life that subtract and add problems to their quality of life. When you meet a guy and within and couple of days or within couple of months, he is asking favors; like borrow your car, borrow

money, stay at your house, get him a cell phone, buy him some new shoes, clothes or games for gaming or ride him different places he is not a plus I your life. Run from situations that don't add much. Good sex should not allow a man to wreck your life and expose your children to possible pedophilia behavior.

You must love your-self more than you love others.

Strong self-esteem helps you to help others.

Don't be afraid of life. Don't be afraid to stand up for yourself. Access your day, week, month, quarter and year. If you were sad more than happy it is time reassess who you have in your life; that includes friend and family member.

Many women with low self-esteem have attracted very bad men that beat them physically

and verbally. This causes problems in the family. I know of cases where the brother was killed or killed the abuser.

You are somebody and should be treated with respect. Don't allow disrespect to dominate your relationship. If he makes to cry, leave.

It is easier to say leave than doing it. You can seek out help from agencies such as women helping women, victims of crimes or other organization in your area.

Learn yourself by yourself. Set some goals in life because if you don't others will use you and find plenty for you to do. Be willing to adjust your goals. Sometimes God has a different plan for you.

When setting your goals be realistic. If your goal is too big, you can get discouraged and never accomplish your goal. Set a realistic time table. And take the first step. Don't share your

dreams and goals with people who are not doing anything. Drop do-nothing people. You need a personal cheerleader. You need to hear you can do it instead, girl let's go get a drink, get high or any other form of wasting time and harming your body with harmful behavior. Watch how you spend your time and who you spend it with. If you do not want to be like the one you are hanging with it's time to change your circle.

Sometimes you have to spend time by yourself to get to know yourself. To build that self-respect and heal from the low self-esteem. Take a step back and remove all distractions. The amount of time depends on the individual and how much growing they have to do. It can range anywhere from 6 month and beyond. Jumping from relationship to relationship is a sign of low self-esteem and the inability to be alone. Always looking for companionship and

happiness in another individual. Learn to receive your happiness from within. Until you learn how to love yourself why would you expect a man to love you. In the process of loving yourself you will learn your self-worth. You will learn exactly what it is you bring to the table and will less likely settle for a man that has nothing to offer you. Your children need a mother who is stable in her decision making as it has a direct impact on not only herself but her children. I know a woman who lacked self-respect and she found herself entangled with a man who didn't respect her let alone her child. He was worse than an Uncle Jerry. She didn't respect herself enough to remove herself from the toxic relationship before it was too late. It cost her the life of her children and herself.

Remember it is your responsibility to protect your children.

Be very careful who you let into your home. Getting children involved in sports, ballet, musical events, drama, and other activities that have coaches or other adult supervision are good ideas but be active in this endeavor, talk to the coaches to feel them out. Don't let the coaches babysit your children, monitor what your children are watching on the media, stop letting the TV babysit. I watched a few cartoons and they are convening bad behaviors, disrespect, raunchy dance moves creating an inappropriate demeanor. It's your responsibility to teach your children in your home about your culture, history, manners, respect, self-respect, self-esteem, respect for others regardless of religion or color. There are many things that are not taught in school such

as social skill and how to love. Sexuality is being taught in school that homosexual life-style is normal. Sexual ordination is a subject for parent to teach or share in a young child's choice in life. Very young children need to be taught early about unwanted touching, feeling and fondling is bad behavior. There were several little boys in my neighborhood that visited an Uncle Jerry and turned out liking other boy and as a result and some became flamboyant homosexuals and other stayed in the closet; ashamed of the hidden secrets, thus an Uncle Jerry is born.

In summary let's discuss how to recognize a Pedophile and what he is seeking:

The Uncle Jerrys of the world have a deep interest in children and have toys, animals, playing

games with children. My Uncle Jerry liked to play ride the horsey. One day he asked me if I wanted the horse to come out the barn. I was very young and noticed the horse was bulging near his zipper. I got scared and told my Aunt, didn't see Uncle Jerry ever again after that. I heard he came back to die with my Aunt but no more riding in his lap and eventually in the bed playing with Uncle Jerry which my Aunt and his wife was just in the other room.

Watch that tickling and going to the store with Uncle Jerry. Never let your child sit in a grown man's lap.

A grown man with toys is suspect.

Always asking about your children and their ages should make you wonder why he is so interested in your children.

Has he shared with you that he was a victim of sexual or emotional abuse?

They seek children that are victims of physical or verbal abuse and are prime for grooming. The first step is usually not physical.

Most pedophiles are not strangers

They seek alone time with your child, offer to babysit, take to store, take to sports events, take to football, baseball or sports practices to help you out.

He likes to take pictures with children

Have a sexual addiction, always wanting sex from you, your child could be next.

You notice some odd behavior from your child, especially around Uncle Jerry.

They are usually an adult male that is married and will give your children money right in front of you.

Watch out for professionals that will groom your children: Minister, Pastors, Bishops, Elders, Deacons, Sunday School teachers, children's

dentist/doctor, Coaches, Teachers, Boy Scout leaders, your neighbor and the one you brought home last night and you introduced as Uncle Jerry. Be careful who you bring home because your children will trust them.

Check your children's underwear to look for semen or blood.

Some phrase I've heard from women of low-esteem say:

"I'd rather have a half a loaf than no loaf at all"

"I know my man is the community man but he comes home to me"

"He has 20 kids but he takes care of mine"

"He hit me because he loves me"

"He didn't mean to hurt my feelings"

"She my wife-in-law" I don't mind sharing as long as I get mine"

"I doing everything for him and he still cheats on me"

"He has to be with his family on holidays. But he spends the night with me" (sometimes)

"I am too fat to be loved" or "I am too ugly to be loved" is signs of low-esteem; you are BEAUTIFUL

Using comfort food to cover up depression and becoming unhealthy is an escape many women use to ease their pain.

The next time you go out and have drinks or drugs don't bring that man home with you around your children. You may be sexually active and have the need and desire for the touch of a man know that he may desire your child. This

is a hard subject but needs to be addressed. The cycle continues in our community because of bad judgement. Most men that conduct this behavior have been victims, too.

Protect the babies. Alcohol and drugs are precursors for sexual abuse. Men use the excuse that "Gin made me Sin", "I was drunk", "I'm sorry I had too much Crack", "I'm Sick" stop excepting excuses. I have counseled women and they said their partner told them they are not homosexual they are freaks. My response is they are freaking homosexual. That type of man should not be around your children. If you smell anal scents while having sex; there is a good chance someone has been having sex in his anal and he likes it both ways. Just because he is having sex with you does not mean he does not want to have sex with men, too. If he begs for anal sex with you, he might be doing anal sex with men. Be careful out there.

In closing I will like to write a letter to the pedophile:

Dear Uncle Jerry (Mr. or Mrs. Pedophile)

I understand you have a sickness. I understand in some cases it was done to you so you are doing it to an innocent child, girl or boy. Remember how you felt as the adult penetrated your innocent soul. Remember the terror you experienced when the perpetrator (a person who carries out a harmful illegal or immortal act) violated your pure body. Know the lifetime harm you are doing to your victim. Seek help, pray and withdraw from your ways. Save a life, stop and ask from forgiven. Your lust for children is unnatural. Sex actually is for procreation only. Humans, pigs, dolphins and baboons (there are 5 species: chacma, olive, guinea, hamadryas, and yellow) have sex for fun, most other species in the animal kingdom have sex for

reproduction. You are a special breed for such an abnormal act. To repeatedly have sex with children can ruins their life as you pleasure yourself; such a selfish act. Know your self-fulfilling behavior is hurting that child. You are creating a monster to unleash on society. If the child is brought up in a very religious environment, they will try to hide their desire and go into the closet in shame. This create a psychological mindset that causes him to interfere with a woman that is seeking love that he can never give. The ramifications have a ripple effect throughout our community.

STOP SEEK HELP